Bees
Wasps

Written by Jo Windsor

Rigby

In this book
you will see bees
and wasps.

You will see...

bees

wasps

stingers

It is summertime.

There is a lot of buzzing.

Buzz, buzz, buzz!

Buzz, buzz, buzz. Is it...

a cat   Yes? No?

a bee   Yes? No?

a snail   Yes? No?

me   Yes? No?

Bees and wasps have wings.

Bees and wasps have eyes.

Bees and wasps have six legs.

Bees and wasps have...

2 legs   Yes? No?

8 legs   Yes? No?

6 legs   Yes? No?

no legs   Yes? No?

wings

eyes

legs

What is this?

Is it a bee or a wasp?

It is **black** and orange.
It has lots and lots of hairs.
It has hairs on its head, too.

Yes, this is a bee.

A wasp is **yellow** and **black**.

There are not so many hairs on its head.

Bees live with lots of bees.

They make nests called hives.
Bees make their nests out of wax.

A nest has lots of rooms.
The rooms have six sides.

Baby bees live in some of the rooms.

This bee is hatching.

room with
six sides

Some wasps live with other wasps.

Wasps get wood to make their nest.
They make the wood into paper.
They make a nest with the paper.

A wasp nest has little rooms.

Some little rooms are for the baby wasps.

baby wasps inside the nest

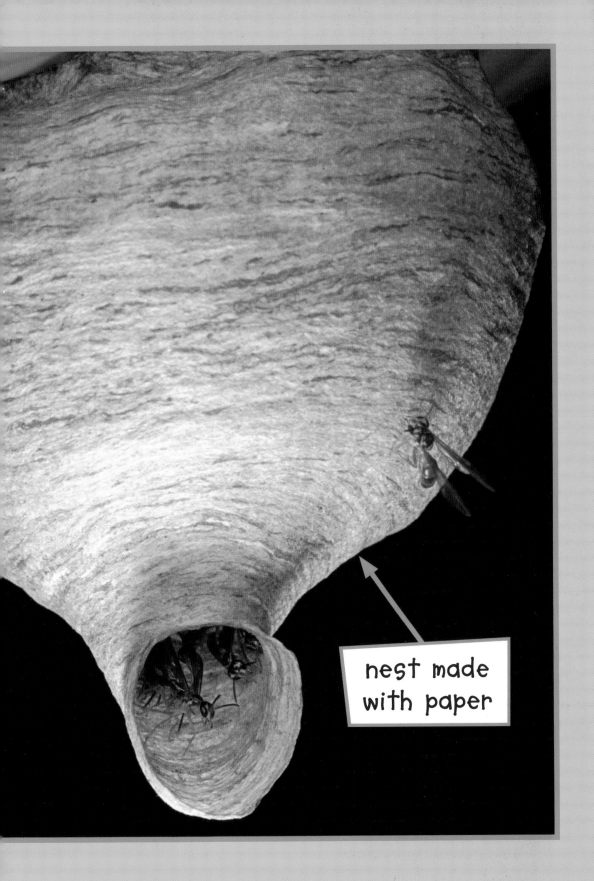

nest made
with paper

Wasps like to catch their food.

They like to eat meat.

A wasp has big jaws.

jaws

A wasp has...

eyes Yes? No?

feathers Yes? No?

jaws Yes? No?

wings Yes? No?

Look at the bee's tongue!

Bees put their tongue
into a flower to get food.

They take the food back to the nest.

They make it into honey.

tongue

Bees get pollen from the flowers, too.

They have bags on their legs.

They put the pollen in the bags.

They take the pollen back to the hive to feed baby bees.

bag of pollen

A bee has a stinger.

The stinger has little hooks on it.

The hooks stick into what the bee stings.

When a bee stings,
the stinger comes out.

The bee dies.

That sting will hurt a lot.

stinger

Look out for wasps!

Wasps can sting
lots and lots of times.

wasp stinger

Index

A yes/no chart

Bee

A bee
can sting.
Yes? No?

A bee has
feathers.
Yes? No?

A bee lives in
a paper nest.
Yes? No?

A bee eats
mice.
Yes? No?

Wasp

A wasp cannot sting. Yes? No?

Wasps have 8 legs. Yes? No?

Wasps live under the ground. Yes? No?

A wasp eats meat. Yes? No?

Word Bank

eyes

hook

flower

legs

hive

wings